PATRICIA SCANLAN

The Bold Bad Girl

With illustrations by Ann Kennedy

Children's
POOLBEG

To Fiona, Caitríona, Laura, John, Jennifer, Catherine, Christopher, Eamonn, Alison, Fionnuala and David

Once upon a time a bold bad girl lived in a little house up the lane. The bold bad girl was very naughty indeed, and her mother didn't know what to do with her. All day long she spent scolding Barbara, for Barbara was the bold bad girl's name.

"Barbara, stop pulling your sister's hair."

"Shan't," said the bold bad girl.

"Barbara, stop scuffing your shoes against the footpath."

"Won't," said the bold bad girl, sticking her tongue out as far as she could.

"Oh, you *are* a bold bad girl," said her mother crossly. "I shall tell your father the minute he comes in."

"See if I care," said bold Barbara, making a face that frightened all the birds and animals down Leafy Lane.

1

"Bold bad Barbara is being cheeky to her mother and pulling her sister's hair and scuffing her shoes along the footpath," Squiffy Squirrel told Robbie Rabbit, as they hid behind a bush.

"That's nothing," exclaimed Terence Tortoise. "Yesterday the bold bad girl pulled a feather out of Maggie Magpie's tail."

"She didn't!" exclaimed Squiffy Squirrel and Robbie Rabbit.

"Oh yes she did," said Terence Tortoise, "and Maggie Magpie was so angry she flew straight off to tell the woodland fairies."

"The woodland fairies!" Squiffy Squirrel and Robbie Rabbit said together as their eyes grew round with wonder. "Oh boy! The bold bad girl is in big trouble now."

The bold bad girl would not eat her tea. She sprinkled pepper into her mashed banana and gave it to her baby sister. The baby's eyes watered and she started to cry. Barbara's mammy came running in.

"What are you doing?" she asked, tasting the peppery banana mash. She made an awful face. "Oh, you are *such* a bold girl, Barbara. Get down from the table immediately and go and get ready for bed. Just wait until your father gets home!"

"See if I care," scowled the bold bad girl. "I want to go out to play. It's much too early to go to bed."

"You are going to bed right now for being such a bold bad girl today," her mother said as she kissed the poor baby. "Look what you did to your poor baby sister. Look what you did to your good new shoes. I've never seen such boldness. Your father will be shocked!"

"Goody," said the bold bad girl wickedly as she gave the cat a kick on her way upstairs to the bathroom.

The bold bad girl filled the washbasin with water and shook a whole tin of talcum powder into the water. It made a terrible mess and turned into a gooey paste. She made horrible faces out of it and stuck in a bar of soap so that it looked like a hideous monster with a green frothy mouth.

"This is good fun," smiled the bold bad girl as she squeezed toothpaste in a blue circle all around her monster's face. A knock on the door made her jump.

"Barbara, come out here, I want to talk to you," said her father sternly.

"Won't," said the bold bad girl. "I'm busy."

"*Immediately,*" said her father in his crossest voice.

She punched her monster in the nose and opened the bathroom door to see her father standing outside looking very cross.

"Mammy tells me you've been a bold bad girl all day," he said.

"Wasn't."

"Don't tell fibs."

The bold bad girl stuck out her tongue as far as it would go.

"Good gracious!" exclaimed her father. "You are certainly a bold bad girl today. There's only one place for you, miss. Into bed immediately. Now get undressed and say your prayers. I don't want to hear another word from you."

The bold bad girl howled and stamped her foot in a mighty rage.

The bold bad girl was feeling very sorry for herself as she sat in her bed looking out the window at the frolics of the woodland animals. She could see Squiffy Squirrel and Robbie Rabbit playing hide-and-go-seek among the trees. Maggie Magpie was admiring her reflection in the rippling water of Willow Pond, and Terence Tortoise and Sammy Snail were having a race down Leafy Lane.

"I'm winning! I'm winning!" Yelled Sammy Snail.

"No you're not," puffed Terence Tortoise as he put on an extra spurt and caught up with his friend.

"It's a draw," announced Carly Caterpillar, who was the finishing line.

"Can't catch me!" said Squiffy Squirrel from his hiding place in the hollow trunk of the old oak tree.

Robbie Rabbit scratched his furry ears. He didn't know where Squiffy Squirrel's voice was coming from. He peered around and saw just the tip of Squiffy Squirrel's bushy tail sticking out of the hollow tree.

"Got you," Robbie laughed happily. "It's my turn to hide now. You count to a hundred."

The bold bad girl gave a great big sigh. It just wasn't fair. She wanted to be out playing hide-and-go-seek. She was a very fast runner. She would easily have beaten Sammy Snail and Terence Tortoise.

She knelt on her bed with her arms on the window-sill, looking very cross. The bold bad girl pushed open the window. Now this was a very naughty thing to do. Her mammy and daddy had told her many times not to open the window because it was dangerous and she might fall out. The bold bad girl peered out the open window. A wicked gleam came into her eye. "I think I'll climb out the window and go and play," she decided.

As bold as you like, she climbed out her bedroom window onto the roof of the front porch and down a drainpipe, and then, with a hasty look around to make sure her parents weren't looking, she ran down Leafy Lane and straight over to the woods.

Poor Terence Tortoise was covered in dust the bold bad girl had kicked up as·she galloped down Leafy Lane.

"She's a very silly girl to be going into the woods when it's getting dark. That's the time that Jinn Jinn is about," he said.

"Oh, don't even mention her name," shuddered Carly Caterpillar. Jinn Jinn was the wicked witch of the woods.

"It's time we were going home," said Sammy Snail nervously. Everyone was really scared of Jinn Jinn the wicked witch.

The bold bad girl never even noticed the sun dipping its golden head in the west as the moon sat up and got ready for work.

Just as the last rays of the sun disappeared, Jinn Jinn the witch yawned and popped the big piece of chewing gum that was stuck to her bedpost into her mouth. Jinn Jinn hated the sun and never ventured out until it had set.

"What mischief can I get up to tonight?" she wondered as she ran her fingers through her black hair to make it stand on end.

"Oh, I am hungry," she thought. "What will I have to eat?" Jinn Jinn jumped out of bed and marched into the kitchen. She lived in a dark gloomy cave full of cobwebs and dust, for she never did any cleaning. She stuck her head in the fridge and pulled out a piece of mouldy cheese. "Oh, yummy," she said, dipping it into a pot of marmalade and devouring it in one gulp.

"Now, what will I wear?" she mused. "My leather trousers and bright pink tee-shirt." Jinn Jinn liked to be in fashion. She spiked her hair, put on purple eye shadow and yellow lipstick, her big knuckleduster ring and earrings and her Doc Martens, and she was ready to go out on the prowl. Jumping on her magic motorbike, Jinn Jinn revved the engine and set off to see what badness she could get up to.

The bold bad girl splashed up and down in a puddle, ruining her good slippers. She didn't care, she was having great fun. She wasn't a bit scared that she was in the dark wood all by herself.

The next moment something zoomed out of the sky, and the bold bad girl's eyes opened wide at the sight.

"Well, well, well, and what are you doing out of bed at this time of night?" Jinn Jinn cackled, putting on her most ferocious face.

"I'm playing," said the bold bad girl, who was not in the least afraid.

"You can't play here. This is my wood at night," said Jinn Jinn crossly.

"Can," said the bold bad girl.

"Can't," said Jinn Jinn in a terrible temper.

"Can so," said the bold bad girl with a scowl.

"Cannot," said Jinn Jinn, driving down on her motorbike and coming to a stop beside the bold bad girl. "I'm going to put a spell on you and bring you back to my cave," said the angry witch as she jumped off her bike and reached out to grab the little girl.

The next minute Jinn Jinn was yelling so loudly it woke up all the woodland animals. "Ouch! Eeek! Aah!" she screeched as the bold bad girl pulled her hair and kicked her on the shins.

As quickly as she could, Jinn Jinn jumped on her bike and flew up into the sky. "I'm telling my mammy on you, you nasty bully!" she bawled, driving home as quickly as she could.

"See if I care," shouted the bold bad girl, throwing a stone after her.

No-one could believe it. The bold bad girl had pulled the wicked Jinn Jinn's hair and sent her scurrying home.

"That showed her," the bold bad girl said, as she wandered deeper into the dark wood. This was an exciting adventure, much better than being in bed.

The bold bad girl skipped along excitedly. Her path was lit by
the bright moon and the Shining Star. She could see a light
through the trees, a strange bright light that outshone even the
moon and Shining Star. The light was getting brighter and brighter.
The bold bad girl peered through the trees. "Ooh!" she exclaimed.
"A fairy fort. This *is* the best adventure!"

In the middle of the clearing she could see a fairy fort all lit up, and from inside she could hear the sound of merry laughter. She crept forward. Beautiful music made her feel like dancing. "I must get in there," she thought. "I want to dance and dance!"

Inside, the most wonderful sight greeted her. In the middle of the room the fairy queen sat on her throne of gold. All around her the woodland fairies danced and sang, as happy as could be.

"Oh, goody, a party!" thought the bold bad girl to herself.

She was just about to move forward to start dancing when a little voice near her ear said, "I'm very sorry, but bold bad girls are not allowed to enter the fairy fort and join our party."

The bold bad girl looked up and saw one of the woodland fairies flying beside her.

"I'm not a bold bad girl and I want to dance!" she exclaimed indignantly.

"I'm very sorry, but today you were a very bold bad girl and you cannot be allowed to stay in our fort and play."

"But I want to!" The bold bad girl stamped her foot in a terrible temper. She barged past and started to run towards the place where all the woodland fairies danced around the queen's throne.

The next minute she found she could not move. She struggled and tried her best, but she just could not budge an inch. She couldn't even talk.

"I'm Fairy Fiona, and I'm going to show you just what a bold bad girl you've been today," the little fairy said.

Fairy Fiona waved her magic wand and the next minute the bold bad girl was turned into her baby sister. Quick as a flash, Fairy Fiona pulled her hair.

"Ouch!" screeched the bold bad girl. "That hurt! I'm telling my mammy on you!"

"Yes, it did hurt, didn't it?" said Fairy Fiona. "That's what you did to your sister today. It wasn't very nice, now was it?"

"I didn't, I didn't!" yelled the bold bad girl as she turned back into herself.

"Don't tell fibs—it's very naughty," Fairy Fiona warned as she waved her magic wand once again.

The bold bad girl found herself turned into Maggie Magpie. The next minute Fairy Fiona plucked a feather out of her tail.

"Ow!" squealed the bold bad girl.

Before she knew what was happening, Fairy Fiona had waved her magic wand and Barbara found herself turned into Terence Tortoise. The next minute she was covered in dust. The bold bad girl spluttered and coughed.

With another wave of the magic wand she was turned into herself again.

"They were only some of the naughty things you did today," Fairy Fiona said sadly.

The bold bad girl was starting to feel very sorry for herself.
"You hurt me," she sniffed.

"I was just showing you what it feels like to have your hair pulled, your feathers plucked, or to be covered in dust like poor Terence Tortoise when you ran down Leafy Lane and he couldn't get out of the way quickly enough. It doesn't feel nice at all, does it?" asked Fairy Fiona sternly. The bold bad girl shook her head.

"Well, just remember how the other person feels before you do something naughty again," Fairy Fiona said softly.

The bold bad girl nodded. She was very tired and her head was sore where her hair had been pulled.

"Would you like to go home?" Fairy Fiona asked.

"Yes, please," said the bold bad girl.

"You won't ever again climb out the window and stay out after dark, will you?" asked the little fairy.

"No, never," said Barbara.

"Promise!" said the fairy.

"I promise," said the little girl.

Fairy Fiona waved her magic wand, and before she knew it, the bold bad girl was back in her own bed tucked up with the moon and Shining Star sending their beams through the window.

"No more naughty deeds, now," smiled Fairy Fiona from the end of the bed. "And if you're a very good girl, I'll bring you to the fairy fort and you can come to our next party. But you must be very *very* good indeed."

"I will be," promised Barbara, giving a big wide yawn. Then she fell fast asleep.

With a wave of her wand, Fairy Fiona flew out the window and back to the fairy fort. All the woodland animals slumbered peacefully in the woods and it would be a long time before the wicked Jinn Jinn dared to show her face again. And all thanks to the bold bad girl, who was going to be a bold bad girl no longer.

First published 1993 by
Poolbeg
A division of Poolbeg Enterprises Ltd
Knocksedan House
123 Baldoyle Industrial Estate, Dublin 13

A catalogue record for this book is available from the British Library.

ISBN 1 85371 266 3

Cover illustration by Ann Kennedy
Cover design by Poolbeg Group Services Ltd
Set by Poolbeg Group Services Ltd
Colour reproduction by Typeform Repro, Dublin
Printed by Colour Books, Baldoyle Industrial Estate, Dublin 13